101 Things to Do with Baby

101 Things to Do with Baby

Jan Ormerod

Groundwood Books / House of Anansi Press
Toronto   Berkeley

1 say good morning

2 play with Baby before breakfast

3 put him in his special chair

4 give him cereal

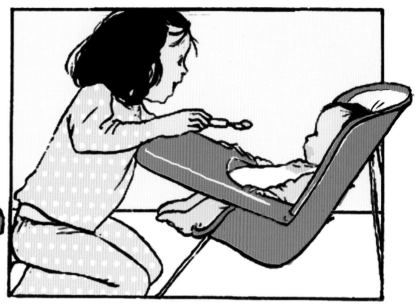

5 and let him share your egg

6 better clean him up

7 let's do the laundry

8 put it in the machine

9 add the soap

10 watch it whiz around

11 spy him with your little eye

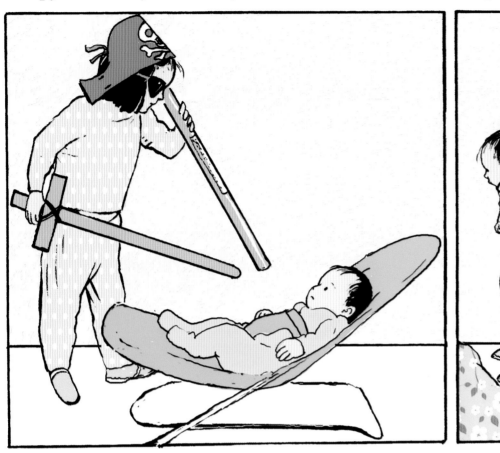

12 put him on the floor

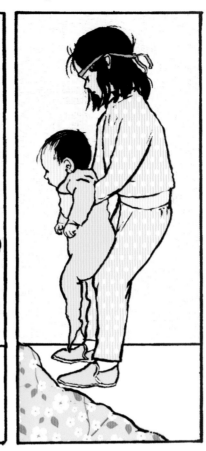

13 for a chat

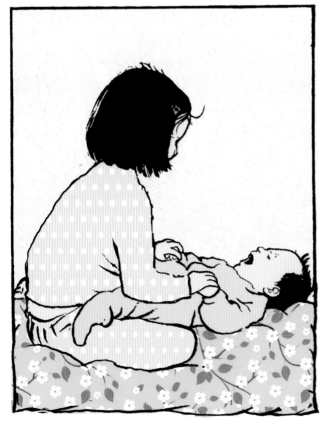

14 exercise his legs

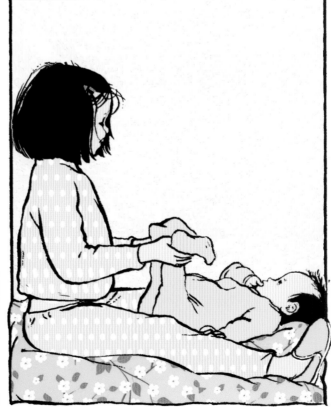

15 now do sit-ups

16 or stand-ups

17 or push-ups

18 see how we can stretch

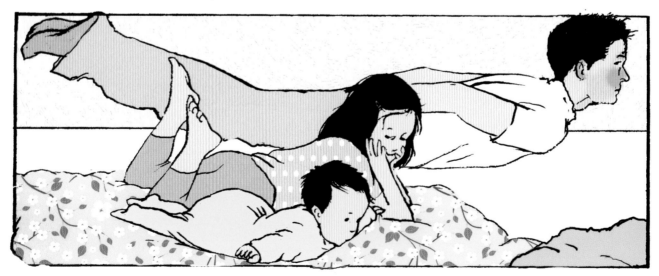

19 twist left

20 twist right

21 and roll over

22 now knees up all together

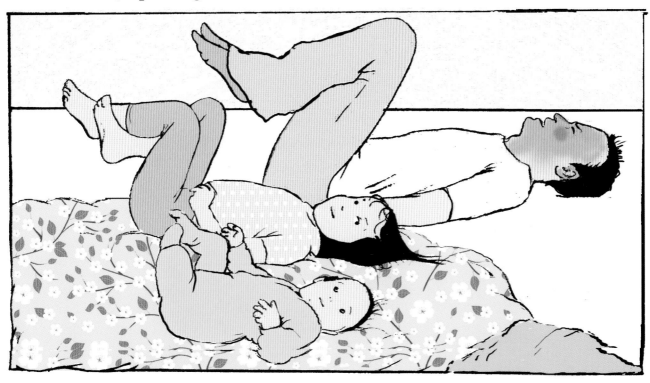

23 and then relax

24 put on rubber boots

25 and a plastic apron

26 get the mop

27 Baby's bath

28 and a nice soft towel

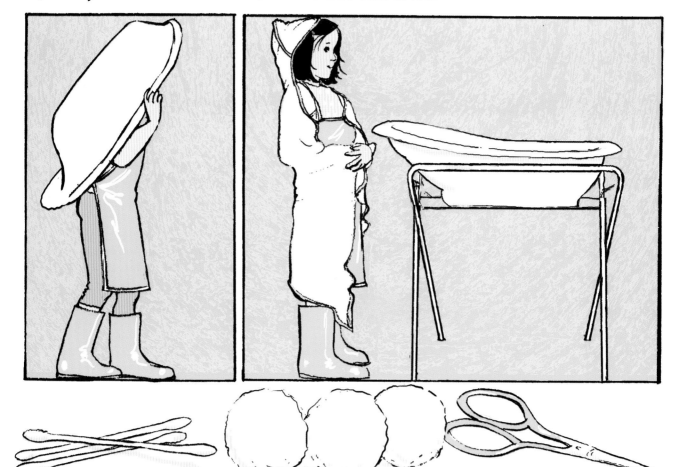

29 not too hot

30 put in the bubbles

31 froth them up

32 put in Baby

33 and dodge the splashes

34 dry him　　35 dress him　　36 brush his hair

37 kiss him better

38 whisper a secret

39 tickle his tummy

40 and give him some toys

watch out for ...

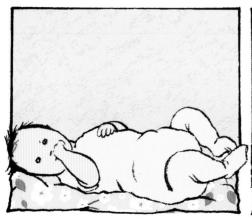

41 hair pulling

42 nose grabbing

43 dribbling

44 and drooling

45 watch out for shoe sucking

46 letter eating

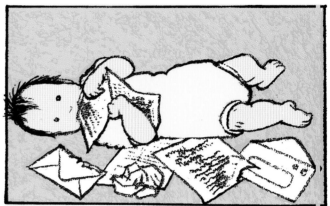

47 ankle biting

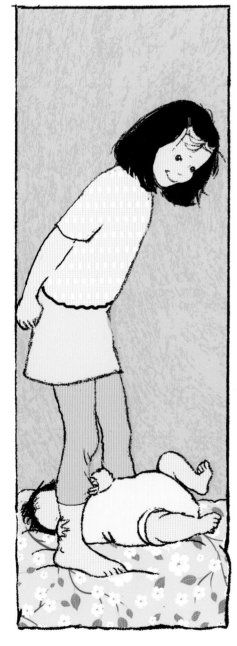

48 head banging

49 and watch out for Granny's glasses

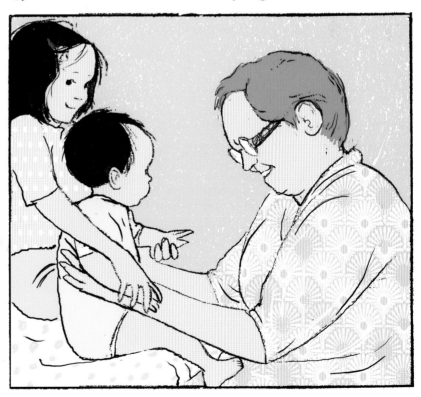

50 hang out the laundry

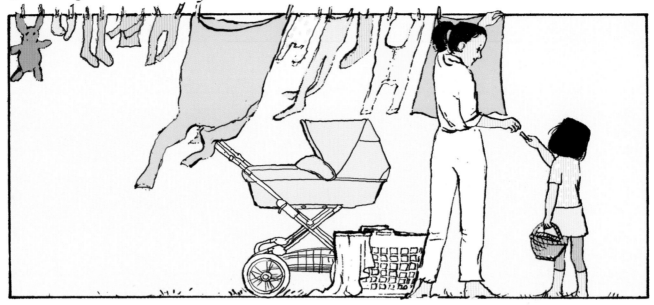

51 rock Baby to sleep

52 shoo away the cat

53 make a daisy chain

54 and look out for rain

55 bring the laundry in again

56 hide

57 say boo

58 play peep

59 try on Mother's hat

60 or Father's shoe

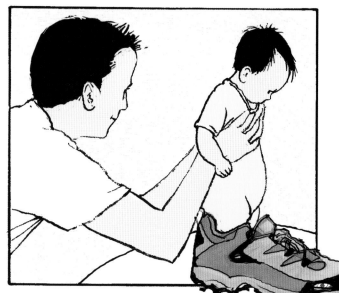

61 put him in his crib
for a quiet time

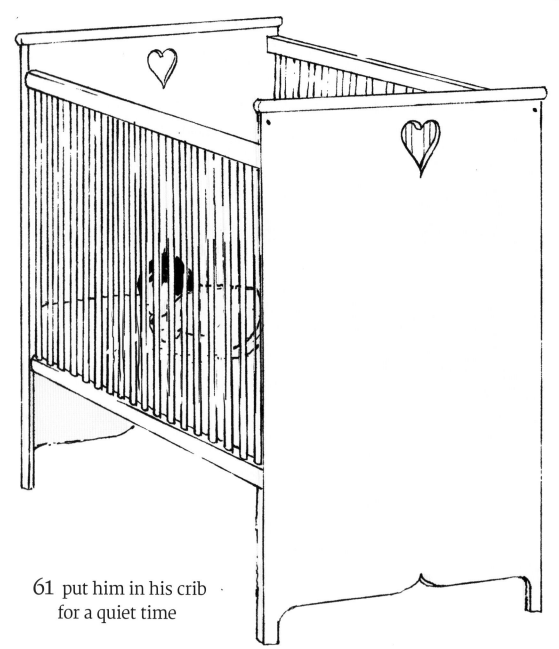

62 dress up in his blanket **63** play with his teddy **64** build with his blocks

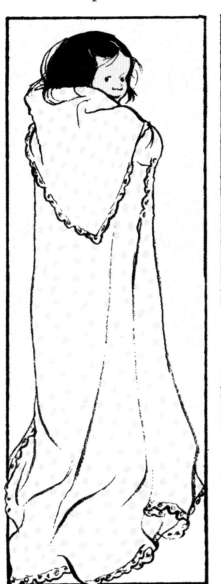  

65 or borrow his basket

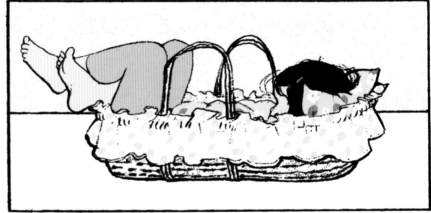

until he wakes up again

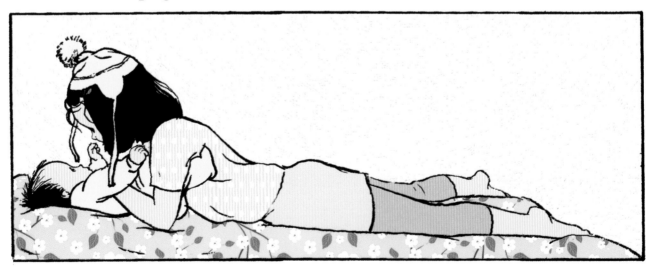

66 touch his nose

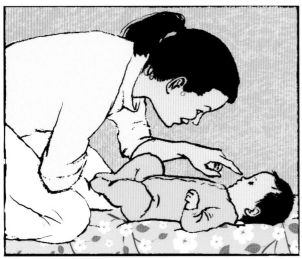

67 walk up from his toes

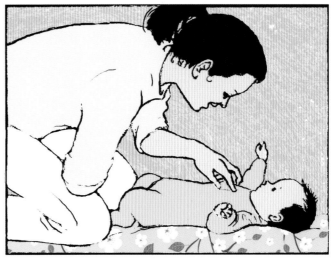

68 kiss his ear or

69 blow on his tummy

72 take him in the car

73 or take him on a picnic

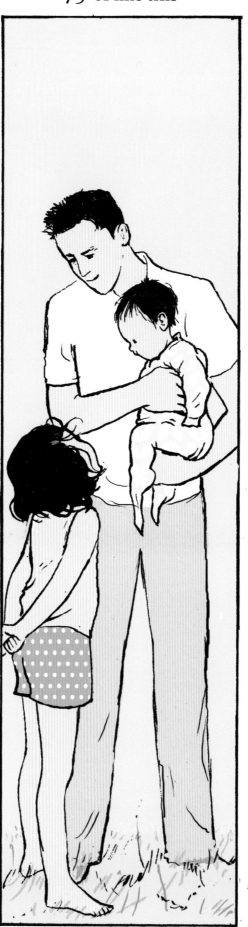

77 or this

78 best like this?

79 no, like this

80 collect rocks 81 leaves 82 bugs

83 and flowers for him but not to eat

84 let him meet big dogs

85 babies

86 snails

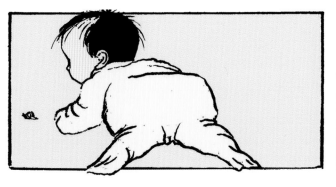

87 and fish

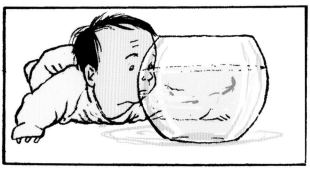

88 roll him up in a rug

89 make him a baby box

90 take him into your tent
with you

91 try him in his bouncy chair

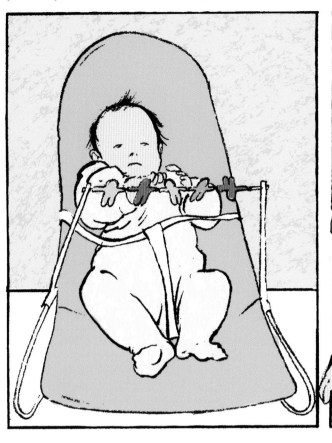

92 try him with a book

93 try him with some rattling toys

94 or let him sit with you

95 watch TV together

until he's bored

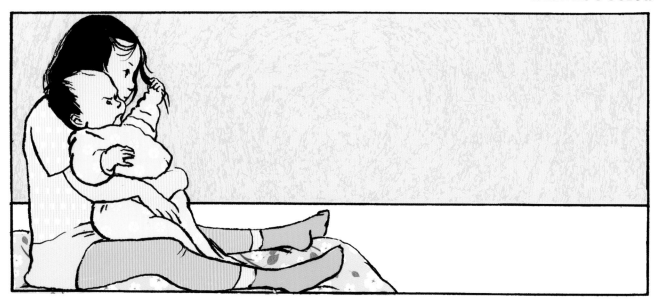

96 give him a book to read

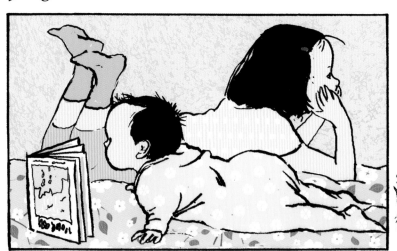

97 but not to chew or tear

98 try not to shout at him

99 and make him cry

100 give him a cuddle

101 and a kiss goodnight

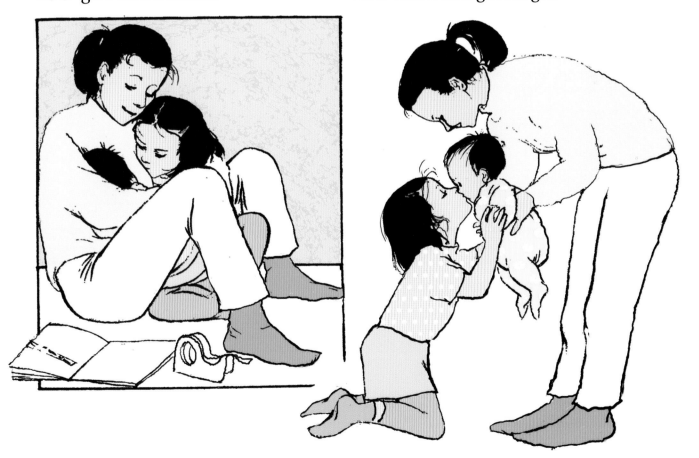

Groundwood Books / House of Anansi Press
110 Spadina Avenue, Suite 801, Toronto, Ontario M5V 2K4
or c/o Publishers Group West
1700 Fourth Street, Berkeley, CA 94710

We acknowledge for their financial support of our publishing program the
Government of Canada through the Canada Book Fund (CBF).

Library and Archives Canada Cataloguing in Publication
Ormerod, Jan
[101 things to do with a baby]
101 things to do with baby / written and illustrated by Jan Ormerod.
Originally published: 101 things to do with a baby / Jan Ormerod. —
London : Kestrel, 1984.
Issued in print and electronic formats.
ISBN 978-1-55498-379-7 (bound). — ISBN 978-1-55498-380-3 (html)
I. Title. II. Title: One hundred and one things to do with baby.
III. Title: 101 things to do with a baby.
PZ7.O650n 2014   j823'.914   C2013-904907-X
C2013-904908-8

Printed and bound in Malaysia

FSC
www.fsc.org
MIX
Paper from
responsible sources
FSC® C012700